The Haunting of Cardon House

©2018 by Carrie Bates

All rights reserved. No part of this may be reproduced, distributed or transmitted in any form or by any means without prior written permission.

This is a work of fiction. Names, characters, places and incidents are a product of the author's imagination. Any resemblance to actual people, living or dead, or to businesses, events or locales is completely coincidental.

Prologue
Chapter 1
Chapter 2
Chapter 3
Chapter 4
Chapter 5
Chapter 6
Chapter 7
Chapter 8
Chapter 9
More Haunted House Books

Prologue

Before the house ever existed, the land was alive with the history of the native people. And, the land was content to be put to use by people who appreciated it – the tribe conducted themselves morally, treating each other and the earth with respect. They gave thanks for everything they took from it, made use of every single berry and bone, and lived a peaceful life in the beautiful wooded area to the north.

They were a serious but friendly people, and when the French trader came down the river in the first few days of spring, they welcomed him as they had all the others before him. He chose to stay and learn their ways of trapping, favoring them over his own. He didn't need to trap to make money – he had behind him a lucrative trading business that he managed by mail. But he wanted a quieter, more content life for himself, and he found what he needed among the tribe.

The natives knew the secrets of the land and the animals he hunted. He took up their habit of thanking the spirits whenever he found a beaver or mink in his traps. It wasn't long before he caught the eye of the fairest woman in the tribe. She was sought after by many of the men, but had turned every single one of them down. She had eyes only for the French trader. He was so well respected that once she made her intentions clear no one objected – not even her father, who currently led the tribe as chief.

It was indisputable that accepting the trader among them had only benefited everyone. He brought trade and good relationships with men who otherwise would've taken advantage of the tribe.

It wasn't long before she bore the trader three children – all boys – and the chief was so proud that he gifted his son-in-law a piece of land of his choosing. The small family was growing quickly, and they needed the room to flourish.

The trader chose a section of land that other white men had tried to purchase before. The tribe had rudely chased all of them off, and they reacted violently when the trader tried to claim this same piece of land. He assumed it was because the land was particularly valuable and took offense, threatening to leave with his wife and sons.

"You don't understand," his wife tried to tell him one night, "We're doing it to keep you safe. That land isn't healthy land."

"Don't be ridiculous," he bit out, pacing the large room they slept in. "That land is flat and fertile. The grass is greener than any in the area, the soil richer – "

"How do you know about the soil?" she asked fearfully, grasping her husband's arms. He stopped, shaking his head at her. Although he respected the tribe, some of their superstitions struck him as too ridiculous.

"I went out two days back and dug down a few feet," he answered. "When you were with the boys."

Her hands dropped to her sides. His wife knew then that there was nothing for it. He'd already tainted himself. She went quietly to her father, who granted his son-in-law the land soon after with the agreement that the couple would continue to live among the tribe and pass on the land to their progeny.

Things were never quite the same after that. Although the grandsons were well-loved and spoiled by their grandfather, the adults in the family had a strained relationship. It continued that way until both the trader and the chief passed away within a few days of one another from old age.

***

Jacques Cardon, a trader like his great-great grandfather, discovered that he'd inherited a piece of land with his father's passing. He set out to see it the day after he received the letter. He had never before heard of it, having grown up in a different state, but traveled to the small town that was just beginning to fill out with a decent population and businesses.

Jacques stood on Main Street watching people walk by, chatting, and as a young boy struggled to haul a sack of flour from the general store, he thought that perhaps he could finally settle down and continue to make a living there. He was already very well-off.

That same day, he made his way to the outskirts of town to see the bundle of land and approved. It was flat and covered in springy, healthy grass and wild flowers.

He spent the night at the only Inn in town. It was there that he saw his future wife – the daughter of the mayor – and thought to himself, drink in hand, that he could *definitely* be happy living there.

Cardon was half French, half Native American, and the latter made the towns people nervous. Tensions with the natives were high. It was said that the surveyors had pushed out the boundaries of the town into tribal territory, and when the natives tried to claim their rightful land, quite a few of them went missing.

But Cardon was a handsome and successful man. All it took was him spending some money in the town, supporting the local businesses, and charming the women. Soon enough, they accepted him as their own and looked past his almond-shaped eyes and beautifully tan skin.

He was betrothed to the mayor's daughter the same week the house was planned to be built. His fiancé, Faith, was a beautiful woman. They were a powerful and promising couple. Cardon opened his own shop with the help of the mayor, a large building right on the main street, and he stocked it well using his connections around the country. Deliveries came in weekly.

It wasn't long until the Cardon's were expecting their first child. Soon, Jacques pulled together a team of men, and the estate was well on its way to being built. He brought Faith out to show her the land, and she immediately started planning for large gardens and walkways.

As soon as the men put the finishing touches on the house – expensive tile floors, the beautifully painted porch, an ornate stained glass window set into the front door – two of Jacques's trading ships went down. Faith found him pacing the back room of his store with the letter gripped tightly in his fist.

"Can't you just contact the merchants in France and get more goods?" Faith asked quietly, cradling her swelling stomach. She'd never seen Jacques like this. The color was rising in his face, turning it a blotchy red, and he grit his teeth.

"You don't understand. It wasn't just the goods on the boat. I sent for the money, too."

"The money?"

"Yes. The money they were keeping for me, from my businesses there. There were three safes on those two ships. That's half of our fortune."

He yanked a chair out from the table and sat abruptly, his head in his hands. "I still need to pay the carpenters for the cabinets and the bed. And…the landscapers. They're still putting in those damned lilac trees you want," he ground out.

"I'm sorry," Faith whispered. The evening was darkening around the edges, and the room was lit by candlelight. The shadows dimmed Jacque's good looks enough that he looked tired and stressed. "The shop is paid off, right?"

Jacques nodded. He'd had enough foresight to buy the shop outright. As long as there were goods in it, they'd have a steady income. "There's another ship coming in three weeks." He sighed, straightening and looked at his wife. Her beauty brought a smile to his face. "We'll have to hold back until then. Just buy food. I'll work something out with the carpenters."

Faith nodded, moving closer to him. He reached a hand out to touch her stomach. "We'll be okay," she murmured, leaning into him.

* * *

But things got worse quickly. Before the third ship had even set sail from France, one of the workers drunkenly lit the Cardon's house on fire when bragging to his saloon buddies that he'd had a hand in building it. A group of them had made their way out to the land, where a lit pipe was dropped onto a pile of landscaping hay.

The house, freshly painted, burned quickly.

The only bit of luck that Jacques had left was that the kitchen was the only part of the house truly gutted. The fire had burned hot enough to leave scorch marks on the new tile, and flames had licked their way up the staircase. The entire first floor would need a thorough cleaning before it was inhabitable.

After that, things went wrong very quickly. Although the store was still stocked, the third ship never showed. Jacques had now gone almost two months without replenishing the goods on the shelves. Frequent customers were bored without new items to browse and purchase.

The messenger found him on a bright afternoon, shuffling through his finance book and adding up numbers. The man was out of breath and haggard. "Cardon," he panted, already turned back toward the door, "Come. Now."

Faith had been visiting her mother and father. She'd gone to the second floor to look at the crib that they'd purchased for their daughter, and she spent quite a while gushing about how beautiful it was. On the way back down the staircase, her foot got caught in the train of her dress. With both hands already on her stomach she was unable to catch herself. There was enough blood that no one had wanted to remove her from the house, but they called the doctor there instead.

They lost the child.

Jacques didn't have time to mourn. Fall was already approaching, and they were behind on paying the bills for construction on the house, without even considering the repairs. He sold his jewelry first, which didn't matter much to him anyway. He was a simple man. It was when he started selling Faith's jewelry without her knowing – she was confined to her bed in a deep depression and ill health – that he took to visiting the saloon in the evenings.

They were told not to try for a child again for at least a year. The foreman leading the team of builders wouldn't begin repairs until Jacques had paid off the original bill. No new goods were coming into the shop, and what was there was old news.

Faith pulled herself from her bedroom after her mother whispered the rumors to her. Jacques drunk every night, the house empty of furniture as he'd had to sell it, his talks to her father about putting the shop up for sale as well. She found him out at the house pacing the lawn in the dark. It was September, and the trees were rattling with what leaves were left clinging to the branches. She shivered, wrapping her coat tighter.

"Jacques," she called, unwilling to step off of the dirt road.

Her husband continued to pace and mutter to himself. She shouted his name again, feeling uneasy in the dark. Her father's porter had dropped her off here and continued on to the post office, where he'd pick up packages, and then return to retrieve her and hopefully Jacques, as well.

"We need to go home," she called, taking one step onto the thick grass. Even now, at night, she was in awe of how beautiful their land was. She could smell the lilacs, which weren't supposed to be blooming now but were heavy with flowers anyway.

Faith never saw Jacques coming up on her despite how large of a man he was. They would find her body first the next day, on the porch. Even as she tried to pry her husband's hands from around her throat, she thought about how strange it was that all of the flowers and bushes were in full bloom in such chill weather.

The porter, who assumed that the couple had left together when he didn't see them waiting that night, found Faith the next morning. It didn't take him long to find Jacques – hanging from an old oak tree in the back yard. He had a flask in his shirt pocket and unpaid bills stuffed into his belt. His handsome face looked grotesque with the noose around his neck and his tongue sticking out.

With no children or relatives, Cardon's home, as destroyed as it was, was given over to the mayor and his wife. They refused to repair it and chose instead to keep it empty.

The town grew bigger. The mayor retired. The house was put up for sale quite a few times, repaired to its original beauty by whatever person owned it for a few months, but never lived in it for long. The owners always seemed to fall on hard times and move on quickly.

Chapter One

Brad and Camille Keeney grinned at one another as soon as they set foot in the foyer. Camille bounced excitedly in place before letting out a squeal and hurrying to see the rest of the house.

She'd only seen the pictures, having had to stay for the sale of their last house as Brad closed on this one, and the woodwork framing of the ceiling was even more beautiful than she'd imagined.

This huge Victorian mansion was going to be their home.

Although still excited, she walked slowly through each room with her chin tilted up. She just could not get over all of the original woodwork and the high ceilings. The windows were huge, the front door even had a section of stained glass, and the yard was meticulously kept despite the property having been on the market for quite a while.

Brad and Camille had seen the listing and fallen in love even as they despaired. The price was relatively low, and they were sure it would fly off the market. But a week later, the house was still listed. Three weeks later, it had even dropped in price…within a month, the couple was preparing their home for sale and negotiating with the realtor in charge of the mansion, who insisted that no one had made an offer yet.

She found Brad standing in the kitchen, hands in his pockets. "Honey?" she asked, still grinning. He turned to smile back at her and held out an arm, wrapping her up against his side.

"Look at this," he said, nodding toward the huge room. Camille searched quickly and couldn't see anything out of the ordinary. Beautiful white tiles and cabinets, large windows letting in the light, newer appliances in spotless stainless steel.

"Mmm?" She bumped up against him, grinning again.

"There," he insisted, removing his arm from around her to point. She followed his gesture and saw it – there, near the door out into the garden, were strange stains seeping up the wall from the floor.

"What is it?" she asked, squinting. Brad walked across the open area and crouched, one hand on the beautiful French doors.

"It looks like…soot, almost. Like something burned here." He stood and began inspecting the rest of the wall. "Weird, though. It isn't anywhere else." He shrugged, turning back to his wife.

"Most of the house is original, right?" Camille asked.

"Well, yeah. Early 1800's. But now that I'm looking at this room, it does seem to be more updated."

"Of course. They had iceboxes in the 1800s, not refrigerators!"

"No, I mean, they would have left the tile original, too. It's not new but it's definitely not that old. And the woodwork, too." He gestured at the beams on the ceiling. "They're definitely newer than the rest. You can tell by the way the paint sits on it."

Camille was squinting again, trying to see the differences her husband was pointing out.

They were both wealthy, but Brad hadn't always been. He came from a family of tradesmen and had worked his way up into the stock industry from the mail room. He had an eye for this kind of stuff.

"All right…well, I'm not that upset. I mean, for a house this old it's in pretty good condition."

"Yeah, it is. The realtor said it hasn't been much lived in."

Camille shrugged. "Works for me. Have you gone upstairs yet?"

Brad grinned, his wife's excitement infectious. "Yeah, I beat you to it. You get first choice for office. The one upstairs is bigger but the one down here opens up into the garden." He wiggled his eyebrows comically at her, and Camille laughed.

She'd been nervous on the drive out from the city. The U-Haul trucks left early in the morning to unload their possessions before they arrived. The furniture was placed almost exactly where she'd imagined it, but they still had boxes of kitchen utensils, clothing, and sentimental items to unpack.

While Brad came from a simple background, Camille did not. She was a city child, and nervous about working from home, even though being a stockbroker of her caliber didn't require working in the city. None of her clients had batted an eyelash when she'd told them she'd be moving two hours away – as long as she had good reception and they could reach her, they were happy.

Brad and Camille made their clients money and put away a good deal for themselves. It was how they'd been able to purchase the mansion, which probably wouldn't have happened if Camille hadn't been so captivated by its beauty. She knew that where she saw offices, Brad saw future bedrooms for their children. The children she wasn't sure she wanted to have.

At thirty, Camille was very young for how far she'd come, and Brad was only two years her senior. She couldn't imagine not focusing on her career, and although Brad got excited about the idea of having kids, he wouldn't be the one having to carry them around for nine months!

He'd gotten her out here, though, and she honestly couldn't be happier. Maybe his plans for the future weren't so bad after all…

Chapter Two

Camille had chosen the office downstairs, which Brad took as a good sign. She'd been particularly resistant to talks of the future lately. But she couldn't resist the beauty of the backyard. Right outside of her office doors was a short walkway to a patio surrounded by flower beds. She was in town for the day, looking for a small table and chair set to put out there so she could have her morning coffee and look at the flowers.

Brad was still in the process of unpacking his own office, but he had the computer set up and had already searched out a few local companies he hoped to work with.

Despite the bathrooms, three of them, all having newer fixtures, the water for the past few mornings had spewed out rusty and loud. The only plumber Brad had known growing up had been his uncle, who he'd never gotten along with, and so he didn't know much about plumbing. Which is why he set out to find a local guy who could come and see what the problem was.

He jotted down the name and number of someone who looked promising – he had good reviews online – and pulled up a program on his computer to start a list of things that needed fixing.

It made sense, he reasoned, since they'd gotten the mansion so cheap. It *was* a mansion, even if it was on the smaller side. Five large bedrooms, a breakfast area as well as a dining room, two patios, the wrap-around porch, six fireplaces, and two rooms for entertaining.

He wasn't really sure how Camille could imagine *not* having a family. There was so much room for just the two of them. But then, she'd come from a household where she'd been the only child, and Brad had two older brothers and four sisters. His aunt and cousin had also lived with the family while growing up, so he was used to little space and a lot of family.

Now, he thought, leaning back in his chair and stretching, he had more than enough room. But he still looked forward to the day when he'd hear laughter out in the hall, see his door creak open to reveal a grin just like Camille's and dark, messy hair similar to his own.

Brad had a very focused mind and that made him good at his job. He and Camille had taken two weeks off to get themselves situated in their new home, and now his only preoccupation was possible repairs in the house.

He wandered throughout the rooms, opening the windows to the fresh spring air. In the front living room he paused, looking out at a stand of lilacs that were somehow already in full bloom. He pushed the windows open as far as they could go, knowing that Camille would love the scent of them in the house.

Next, he went to each faucet, turning it on and waiting to see how long the water ran rusty for. All of them did to some extent, but it was the worst in his own bathroom. He stood in front of the tap glancing at his watch and the beads of red water striking the porcelain. It took just over six minutes for the water to clear, and even then it sputtered. He definitely wanted the plumber here in the next day or two.

Brad heard Camille call his name from downstairs, and he took his time going down. He found her in the foyer with a large box propped up against her hip. She smiled up at him.

"Could you help me with the chairs?" she asked. "They're in the back of the SUV. The guys at the shop helped me load them, but there's no way I can get them out by myself."

Brad slipped by her as she lugged the box through the house, toward her office in the back and the patio doors she'd left open. He popped open the back of their Lexus and admired the ironwork of the chairs she'd chosen, frowning when he noticed there were only two.

"What if we have guests?" he called to her as he carried them out to where she stood next to the table, hands on her hips. Camille glanced at him. She knew he wasn't talking about guests, but kids.

"We can entertain them out on the other patio. It's bigger, anyway."

Brad grunted and put the chairs down.

The couple spent the rest of the day unpacking the kitchen, laughing and arguing about what should go where. They left the delicate porch lights on when night fell, and Brad grabbed Camille by the waist to sway with her comically in the living room.

She jokingly tried to pry herself away from him, but eventually gave in and rested her head on his chest.

"You should have someone look at that," she murmured, sounding drowsy.

"Look at what?" he asked.

"The light switch. I think it shorted when I turned it off. You didn't see the spark?"

She felt Brad shake his head against her hair, which she had up in a messy bun. "I'm just worried," she continued. "Remember that brownstone down the street from us? The one that caught fire because the wires were old?"

"I do," he murmured, already adding *electrician* to the list in his mind. "The paint is fresh and so are the fixtures, but the bones are old."

"And beautiful," Camille insisted, lifting her head to smile at him.

He smiled back. "I'll call someone tomorrow."

Chapter Three

Almost everything was unpacked, and they still had a week and a half to enjoy before they started reaching out to clients to discuss their investments. Although Camille loved every inch of the house, she particularly loved her office, and broke one of her long-time rules; she put a comfortable loveseat in the corner where she could sink in with a good book. Usually, she liked to keep her work environment strictly professional. But she couldn't help herself.

On Thursday, she could hear Brad's and the plumber's muffled voices from upstairs. The man had already been over twice, sure both times that he'd fixed the rusty water, but it seemed to return as soon as he left.

Camille was tucked away in the loveseat, gazing out the large French doors into the back yard. It was like having a wall of windows. She was contemplating what kind of curtains to hang there, if any at all, when the tree caught her eye.

It was out past the patio and to the left. The immediate area around it was well-kept but void of flowers or other saplings. The tree was old, obviously, and impressively huge. In the city, she'd always admired any tree that managed to grow old enough to get gnarled.

Over the next few days, she wasn't impressed so much as uneasy. A few times, she'd fallen asleep in the loveseat and woken up at dusk to see the silhouette of the tree, terrifyingly huge and twisted. It made her so uncomfortable that she no longer stayed in the office past sundown.

***

With two days left of their mini vacation, Brad was working with the electrician now. Camille was left to her own devices. She wandered the yard, trying to identify flowers she'd never seen before. As a city girl, she really didn't know much about them.

The scent of the lilacs, which were still somehow in full bloom, drew her to the back edge of the yard. It was a few moments before she realized how near to the tree she was. She'd been curling her toes in the luscious grass when, noticing that it was suddenly broken up by large roots, she looked up to find herself under the far-reaching branches.

The tree was so big that being underneath it was like being in a dark room. Camille was caught off guard, imagining for a moment the body of a man hanging from one of the lower branches.

She gasped and stumbled back, her heel catching on a root. Camille scrambled backward into the sunlight, staring up at the tree, Brad's name on her lips.

She searched the branches for a body. Her chest was heaving. The spring sunlight was strengthening finally, and it warmed her back. She glanced back toward the house, then at the tree again.

No man was hanging from that branch. It was twisted, yes, grotesquely so. She got up and hurried toward the house anyway, feeling lightheaded.

Chapter Four

The house seemed to feed off of Brad and Camille's energy.

For the first few months, it felt warm and charming, despite being so large. They had friends and family over for a house warming. Brad spent the evening in deep conversation with his male family members about the work that the plumber and electrician had done. His father even ducked under their master bathroom sink to get a look at the new, high-end pipe system the man had put in.

Camille was absolutely glowing – showing her parents around, catering to her friends, laughing. The two caught each other's eyes across the room and fell a little more in love.

But well into summer, the house became too hot and tense. Camille had begun making the two hour drive into the city twice a week, unable to stay away from the hustle and bustle for too long. At least that was what Brad believed, but he didn't know her true motives. She was uncomfortable sometimes even when Brad was just upstairs in his office. She didn't like looking out into the back yard anymore and began taking her coffee in the breakfast area just off of the kitchen.

She was also completely baffled that the lilacs were still blooming. "The soil is fertile," Brad suggested, shrugging it off. Camille didn't know much about plants, but she was pretty sure that any kind of shrub that flowered didn't last very long. She'd grown up in a brownstone with azaleas out front, and her father regularly commented on how beautiful but short-lived they were.

Brad was waiting for Camille when she got home. He'd heard, second-hand from a client, that she'd lost a big investment, and he wasn't happy.

He couldn't be too upset as his own work wasn't going so well. In the last few weeks, he'd lost a good sum of money on bad investments. But Camille's loss was larger monetarily.

"Maybe," he said dangerously low, "If you didn't spend so much time driving back and forth, and focused on the actual *stocks…*"

"Oh, like you've been doing so great," Camille hissed, throwing her purse onto the counter. "Don't think I didn't see your numbers. Four-point-eight million dollars in a week and a half, Brad?"

"That's nothing compared to what you did this afternoon! What you lost!"

They continued to argue, the house echoing with their shouts, moving from room to room. Brad kicked over the tall chairs in the breakfast nook, and Camille stomped heavily upstairs, glaring as she passed his office.

"If you were *home* more," he insisted, "we could discuss things! We used to talk these things out, Camille, bounce ideas off of each other. You were so excited to come here and now you're gone twice a week. You're not even in your office anymore when I need you…"

Camille was about to argue back when a shadow by the door caused her to stop abruptly. Brad was somewhere behind her, gesticulating angrily, throwing the clean laundry onto the bed. He didn't see the man in the doorway – the way his grimy hair hung down around his face, dirt smudged on his high cheekbones. He was wheezing heavily as he watched the couple, his eyes dark and sunken.

Camille squeaked and stumbled back into the bedroom, bumping into Brad. She turned even as he was still ranting at her and wrapped her arms around his waist, holding tight when he tried to pry her off.

"What are you doing!? Camille."

"There's a man in the hall," she insisted, tightening her hold on her husband and turning so that her back was no longer facing the doorway. "Get him out of the house!"

Brad froze, suddenly unsure. He gripped Camille's shoulders and moved her behind him. In two large strides, he was at the doorway with his arms tense, ready to lash out.

Camille shook as she stared at his broad back. She watched the muscles relax. He looked over his shoulder at her.

"Do you think this is funny?" he asked quietly. "Explain to me…how you don't *want* children, but you have no problem acting like one." The venom in his words made Camille flinch. He was quieter, but angrier. "This conversation isn't over, Camille. You should stay home tomorrow and look over the stocks. Figure out how to get that money back."

With that, Brad left the room and thundered downstairs. Camille knew that he was probably going for the bottle of whiskey that had recently taken up residence in one of their cabinets. She sat at the edge of the bed, arms wrapped tightly around herself, still too scared to step out into the hallway.

Chapter Five

They never recovered the full amount of money lost, but for a short time, it seemed as though their poor luck was plateauing. They neither earned nor lost money. They neither earned nor lost clients. Everything was stagnant.

Despite Brad's words, they never picked up the argument again. Camille went into the city only once a week – she couldn't let go of her office there, but she also couldn't justify paying for it and not spending some time there. At home, she took to carrying her laptop out into the kitchen and working as she baked. It was a new hobby she'd taken up, one that calmed her down.

At first, Brad seemed unsure of how to feel about the muffins and cookies that she churned out. But he hoped, secretly, that she was feeling a bit more at home and comfortable there. More like settling in for the long haul. After all, he couldn't eat all of these baked goods by himself.

Toward the end of summer, as the days grew shorter, Camille spent more time sleeping in. At first, she tried to tell herself that it was the change in daylight that tired her. But she recognized the signs soon enough.

Brad knew what was going on right away, of course, as soon as she missed the first day of work in the city and spent the morning in the bathroom. He managed to contain his excitement until she brought it up – and even then, he waited to see how she reacted.

"I'm pregnant," she said softly. She wrapped her hands around the cup of ginger tea she was nursing, hoping that it would calm her stomach.

They sat out at the larger patio, which Camille preferred now, even though there were less flowers there. There shouldn't be this many flowers at all, she was pretty sure her father had commented on it during his last visit.

The lilacs had finally stopped blooming, but the air still smelled of them. Camille leaned back in the chair and reached out to touch a rose where it tumbled over the patio bricks. She glanced back at Brad, who had schooled his expression to stay neutral.

"You can be happy," she said in an amused voice, but it only made Brad appear more serious.

"I want *you* to be happy," he said, searching her face. She sighed.

"I'm not unhappy, Brad. I just thought I'd have a bit more time to focus on my career." She put a hand unconsciously on her lower belly.

Brad leaned forward and touched her knee. "If you're worried about finances, you don't have to be," he assured her. "Everything has straightened out more or less. We're in a good spot. I know we weren't planning on this, but…I think you'll make a great mother." He said it quietly, and a smile bloomed on Camille's face. She couldn't help feeling warm at his words.

The next day, Brad drove into the city to collect the things she needed from the office. They decided to keep paying the rent, but have Camille work at home, at least until the morning sickness passed.

She wasn't showing at all yet but she very distinctly missed getting her period, and often felt lethargic. She was already sleeping in a lot. Brad let her – their bedroom was two doors down from his office upstairs, and he made sure to shut his door and speak quietly on the phone.

Camille was drowsing in bed one day, listening to her husband's voice, half-drowsing, when a loud voice broke through.

"GET OUT!" it shouted, filling the room.

Camille bolted upright, already putting her arms protectively over her stomach. She could feel the anger and malevolence in the room. The windows were shut – the night air was colder now, and Brad didn't want her catching a chill – it made everything in the room feel more intense.

There were no other words, but Camille heard a growl very close by. She scooted herself back against the headboard, searching the room.

Fear made her spine tingle and suppressed the nausea she usually felt.

She was sure that the voice had come from somewhere near the walk-in closet. With a sudden burst of bravery and protectiveness, she wrapped the sheet around herself and bolted from the room, hurrying down the stairs.

Camille chose not to say anything to Brad about the incident. She spent the afternoon in the kitchen, shakily working on a bundt cake. Her husband had already suggested going to therapy so that she transitioned smoothly from full-time work to motherhood. She didn't want to give him more reason to get her into a therapist's office, which she thought would be both a waste of time and money.

Instead, she swallowed her fear and tried to convince herself that the voice had just been the product of a bad dream, lingering as she let herself doze.

Chapter Six

Over the next few weeks, Camille dreamt of the angry man more and more often.

He was both handsome and terrifying. His features were fine, his eyes a beautiful hue of red-brown, but always, he was howling for her in her dreams. Camille woke each morning with her arms wrapped around her abdomen and the small bump that grew there. She stayed buried in the plush covers long into the afternoon, and her clients began to call Brad when she stopped communicating with them.

Brad was a mess. Reacting to her constant fear and avoidance, which he couldn't understand, he often struck out angrily – only shouting, but Camille was a petite woman and had never seen her husband act this way. Her cowering only made him angrier. Why couldn't she be happy that they were well on their way to becoming a family?

Some days were good days for both of them. She'd get up relatively early and tiptoe downstairs, where she could hear him on the phone with her mother, pleading for advice. Her parents were ecstatic that she was pregnant. And now that she'd gotten used to the idea, she was happy, too. But she was also terrified that something might harm her and the baby.

On one of the good days, they sat eating dinner in the dining room, side by side at their enormous table. Anything smaller would have looked ridiculous in the room.

"I think," Brad began, setting down his silverware, "that you should let me take over most of your clients. Just the small ones," he went on, expecting her to protest. "You have your hands full enough. Let me take care of the minor accounts. You focus on the big guys. You were always better at talking them into investments." He smiled at her, remembering back when they first met, how taken he'd been by her ability to persuade people on almost any topic.

Camille was frowning, gazing off into space. She considered his offer very seriously. Camille was never one to give up on her work, but this would only be temporary. And she *did* have a lot to do, preparing the bedroom next to theirs for the baby. She already had a rocking chair and changing table picked out. Everything would be teal and honey-colored. And…she wouldn't have to spend time in the office anymore. She could easily handle her bigger clients just a day or two a week, a few phone calls made in the kitchen.

"All right," she agreed, smiling back at Brad, who smiled even wider. When things were like this – when they could easily discuss the future and the best way to go about things – they each fell a little more in love with one another.

But that didn't always last.

As Camille was well into the first trimester, she spent her time doing chores and crying randomly. No matter how calmly Brad spoke to her, she couldn't help feeling that they were growing apart. At night he slept on his side, facing away from her, and he grew annoyed whenever she backed up against him, afraid to fall asleep.

"Stop being ridiculous," was something he said a lot these days. Camille kept crying, and he kept storming around upstairs, angry and unable to understand what the problem was.

One afternoon when it smelled like snow in the air, Camille was carrying the basket of laundry downstairs. She wore a huge over-sized sweatshirt, white jersey shorts, and fluffy socks. Altogether, she knew she looked ridiculous, but Brad had commented earlier that she was cute, and it had brought a little happiness to her morning.

Just six steps away from the first floor landing, Camille gasped, feeling large hands grip her shoulders and push. She didn't have time to reach out and try to grab the railing. Instead, she tumbled over the laundry basket, arms wrapped around her middle, shouting for Brad.

It wasn't that far of a fall. But the push had added extra force.

When Brad came running down the stairs, he found Camille howling in pain, clutching a dislocated shoulder. He moved around her quickly, speaking words of reassurance.

Then he saw the blood. It was seeping quickly through her white shorts and onto the soiled clothes strewn everywhere. He froze.

"Brad," she gasped, trying to turn herself so that she could see him. Her husband bolted into the kitchen for the phone and dialed 911 immediately.

Chapter Seven

The days that followed were hard for them both, but strangely enough, the tragedy drew them back together. They needed each other to get through this. And Camille was more open now – she talked to Brad quietly about how, when she was better, she wanted to try again. Losing a child had made her realize how much she really wanted one.

She still slept in most mornings, but was slowly getting back to her work routine. She even made one or two trips into the city to collect her things and end the lease on the office. Brad drove her there, and on the way back out to the country, she asked if he could stop at a store where she bought long black-out curtains that she hung in her home office so that she couldn't see into the back yard.

She wasn't allowed to stretch or do too much physical activity, so Brad was reaching up to put the curtains up as she stared out into the dark.

"I think we should get that tree cut down," she said firmly. One of her hands ghosted across her stomach. Brad looked from his wife to the old gnarled oak in the yard.

"Any particular reason?" he asked, even though he would do anything for her. She was very pale and quieter than she ever had been. He just wanted to see her get better.

"It's a hazard," she said, turning away from the window. "The branches reach out over the area where we wanted to put the garden shed.

It would only take one good storm for that thing to come down. And if – if we have kids…"

She trailed off, but Brad nodded. Back when he'd come to see the house without her, he had imagined putting a swing up on one of those big branches. But he could see why she was worried, and readily agreed.

"I'll call someone in the morning," he said, putting a hand on her lower back as they walked from the room to the staircase.

Camille put a hand on the railing and shivered. It took another reassuring touch from Brad for her to make her way upstairs and to bed.

* * *

Later that night, Camille woke up gasping.

She'd been dreaming that she couldn't breathe – but it wasn't just a dream. She woke to hands tight around her throat, her mouth already wide open trying to suck in air.

She tried to kick and found that there was a heavy weight on top of her. Eyes wide, she stared up into the face of a man – a handsome man.

Her mind went immediately to the man she hadn't seen or dreamt of since the miscarriage. Was he back?

But no – it was Brad. He shifted over her, and she recognized his determined mouth and striking eyes. He was staring down at her, the muscles in his arms flexing as he tightened his hold on her throat.

"Brad!" she choked out, tilting her head back to try and get more air in. The crazed, lustful look in his eyes only intensified. She'd never seen him like this. He was always gentle with her, even when they were messing around, even when they were passionate.

Brad's hair, which had grown out in neglect, hung over his forehead and into his eyes. It obscured his gaze long enough that he removed one hand to push it back, and then she saw the hopelessness there.

"Brad," she choked out again, hoping to reach him in this moment of despair. "Brad, it's me. It's Cam..ille…"

Her vision was starting to darken. She stopped struggling, confused but tired. Just as she was giving in to the fuzziness, Brad's fingers loosened, and he gasped out her name.

"Oh, god," he moaned, gathering her up and pulling her to his chest. She struggled briefly, still scared of him, and he scrambled back from her. "Oh god Camille, I'm so sorry. I don't know what came over me!"

He was crouched on the bed, his pajamas wrinkled and his hair disheveled. He ran a hand through it, shaking his head. "I'm so sorry," he repeated, gripping the comforter tight in his hands.

Camille had her own hand at her throat, gasping in air as her heart rate went back to normal. She stared at her husband. Just moments ago, he hadn't seemed himself, even if he'd looked it. Brad would have never put his hands on her. They'd been married eight years, together for fifteen, and she'd never seen an ounce of violence in him.

She had a decision to make as she sat across from him, watching him break down. She could either move further away and alienate him, or go to him and soothe him.

Camille scooted forward and reached out to put her palm on his knee. He searched her face, making sure she was okay before wrapping a hand around her wrist and pulling her close gently.

"I'm sorry," he started to say again, quietly, but he was interrupted by a deep growl.

Camille froze, the hair on the back of her neck standing on end. She felt Brad stiffen in her arms. They both looked to the far corner of the room, where the sound had come from, and as soon as they saw the dark form there, Brad turned himself so that he was between the figure and his wife.

"Camille," he said quietly, in warning, but the figure was moving quickly – it scrambled up the wall and onto the ceiling. Brad pushed Camille back, keeping his body over her own protectively, caging her in against the mattress.

As it reached the area of the ceiling over the bed, the shadow took a more definite shape. It was a man. As large as Brad, but leaner, clinging to the ceiling and baring his teeth at them. Camille recognized the handsome, repulsive face immediately.

"It's him," she gasped quietly, her fingernails biting into Brad's bicep. They both felt the pressure in the room. If they didn't leave now, whatever this was, was going to kill them.

Without speaking, Brad catapulted off the bed and pulled Camille's petite frame into his arms. He rushed her from the room and down the stairway, prying open the front door. They both bolted across the yard to the SUV, peeling out of the driveway and heading toward the city.

Chapter Eight

Camille was the first to return to the town a week later.

A neighbor had called Brad to let him know that he'd seen the front door wide open when out at the mailbox, and had gone over to lock and close it. Brad thanked him, but let him know that they'd be out of town for quite some time.

They rented a hotel suite and spent days pacing the luxurious rooms, trying to cope with what they'd experienced. Brad eventually had to get back to work calling clients and letting them know how their investments were doing. It was when he was catching up on these calls that Camille swiped the keys, got in the car, and drove back to the small town they'd come to love.

She didn't go back to the house. Instead, she took a right off of Main Street and headed toward the library.

It was an old, old building that the plaque out front identified as the house of the original mayor. The woodwork inside reminded her of the mansion, and she found it both beautiful and terrifying. Standing under one particularly ornate archway, she shivered.

"Can I help you?" someone asked, and Camille turned to see an older woman in spectacles waiting patiently near a desk. She appeared to be checking in books.

"Um, I think so," Camille answered, moving toward the desk. She leaned against it to rest. Her body was still tired from the miscarriage and the trauma of whatever had tried to corner them in the house earlier that week. Even though she trusted Brad, she wasn't yet sleeping easily next to him.

"My husband and I bought a house in town last spring, and we wanted to know a bit more about the history."

"Of the house, or the town?" the woman asked, putting down her books.

"Well…both, I suppose, if you can tell me anything about the house. It's very old, I think."

The woman smiled at her and came fully around the desk. She was taller than Camille but wiry. She wore no wedding ring, and moved confidently toward an area where tables were spread out comfortably for the patrons.

"Which house was it that you bought?" she asked, winding her way through the tables. Camille followed closely.

"The one on Birch Ave. With the yellow door and the lilacs in the yard."

"Ahh," the librarian said, smiling. "I've always loved that house. Even thought about buying it a few years back when it was on the market again. But town jobs don't pay what they used to, and I figured it would be for sale again soon enough."

"What makes you say that?" Camille asked, frowning. Even after being chased from her own house, she wasn't yet willing to part with it.

"It's always been on and off the market. Before you bought it, the previous owners only lived there for two months. The husband…well, they had a turn of bad luck, and he just couldn't forgive himself. He took his own life."

"Not…in the back yard?" Camille asked, her memory flashing back to the man hanging in the tree. The librarian eyed her.

"No, not in the back yard. I don't even think he was at the house. They found him in his car out at the lake. He'd left a note on the counter for his wife, though."

"Oh. My husband never mentioned that, the realtor must not have told him."

The librarian shook her head. They'd stopped in front of a tall, dark bookshelf. "No, she must have notified him. It's the law."

"Maybe he…forgot to tell me," Camille amended, though both she and the woman knew that wasn't the truth. She'd be asking him about that later, when she returned to the hotel. "And the house was on the market a lot before that?"

"Yes, very often. I think the longest it's ever been owned was about two years. But to be honest, I can't tell you much more than that. Very few documents remain after the fire that happened in 1888, but luckily, we have books written about the town history." She gestured to the shelf, smiling, and Camille leaned forward to look.

A few books were about local artists or writers. Some were on the architecture, others specifically about family lineages. Camille thanked the woman and squatted down to search the shelf in earnest.

After a few minutes, she found a thick, older, red-bound book about the general history of the town. It was heavy in her hands as she stood, and she turned to find a table.

Camille leafed through the first few pages, looking mostly at the photos. The book was just over two-hundred pages long. When she didn't recognize any of the houses pictured as her own, she went back to the beginning and sighed.

Before she'd even gotten past the introduction, she found what she was looking for.

The book dove immediately into the origin of the town land. Camille's eyes widened as she read. She picked the book up, careful to keep her place, and moved back toward the desk where the woman was now leafing through some paperwork.

"Excuse me," she said quietly, smiling when the librarian looked up, "I just wanted to check…this book says the entire town was originally lived on by the Sioux?"

"Oh, yes," the librarian answered, brightening. "Before the genocides and the assimilation, this was all native territory. The Sioux here were lucky, though. The land was bought mostly by French traders who they got along with well."

"And this map here – is it accurate?" asked Camille, turning the book so that the librarian could see as she leaned over the desk. The woman studied the old, thin paper, eyes pinched. She backed up a bit, glancing at Camille.

"Uh…yes. Yes, that's definitely correct. I recognize this map from the town records. It's the agreed upon measurements for the layout of the town."

Camille was breathing quickly, her chest heaving. She closed her eyes briefly. In her pocket her phone vibrated, and she was sure that it was Brad looking for her. He could wait. At the moment, she wasn't in the right mindset to talk to him. She could feel anger rising in her chest.

"You're sure?" she asked, fingers still holding down the map, eyes boring into the librarian. "Because if this map is right, then my house is on burial ground."

The librarian cleared her throat, clearly uncomfortable. "Well, yes," she said, pointing down at the inked paper. "Not the regular burial ground, though, that was listed as a protected part of town history twelve years ago…"

"I know," Camille interrupted. "Just tell me. Is this the same area where my house is, now?"

The woman was staring down at the map. She pushed her hair back from her face, where it suddenly stuck to a thin sheen of sweat. "Yes," she answered. "Your house is on the burial ground for the criminally insane. The tribe didn't call them that, of course. To them it was sacred ground – even if the people buried there committed terrible crimes." She glanced up at Camille. "I'm not usually superstitious but…it explains a lot."

"It does," Camille commented quietly, but her mind was elsewhere. She was thinking of Brad. She met the librarian's eyes. "Would my husband have known about this?" she asked, her hand going to their plot of land on the map.

The woman shook her head. "No. The town doesn't usually give the history of a residential building unless the owners come looking for it. And they keep all of the records here, in the basement, not at town hall." She paused, eyeing Camille. "The realtor would have told him about the suicide, though. Even if it didn't happen at the house. I know her – Meg Forbes. She's a notorious gossip. She would've let that slip before they even set foot in the house, I imagine."

* * *

Camille was fuming on the drive back to the hotel. She took corners a bit too fast, and played out the conversation she planned on having with Brad as soon as she got back. Her cell kept pinging, and she knew it was him calling.

He was at the door as soon as he heard her come in.

"Where were you?" he asked, clearly worried. "I've been calling you all morning."

"I went back to town," she bit out, throwing her purse in a chair. Brad's eyes widened.

"You didn't go back to the house…?"

"No, I didn't go back to the house. But you should have mentioned what happened there, Brad."

She watched her husband's face tinge pink. He didn't meet her eyes.

"I know about the suicide," she continued. "The man who lived there before us. Why didn't you say anything?"

He shrugged. "Honestly…I didn't think it was that important. It didn't happen *there,* and the house was so beautiful, I knew you would fall in love with it." He stepped forward, reaching out for her. "I'm sorry Camille. I was just trying to make you happy. And make a home for us."

All at once her annoyance dissipated. She softened in her husband's arms, breathing him in. "You should have told me," she murmured.

He rubbed his chin against the top of her head. "How'd you even find out about it?"

Remembering what else she'd discovered, she stepped back to look up at him. "I went to the library. The librarian showed me this book on the local history. You're not going to believe what that house is sitting on, Brad."

Brad accepted the truth much quicker than Camille did. He'd grown up in a house full of superstitions, his mother throwing salt over her shoulder whenever she dropped it, his father stepping purposefully over the crack in the doorway. "That explains a lot," he muttered, sitting on the edge of the bed. "I'm surprised anyone even thought to build a house there.

There are areas all over the country that tribes still protect because their dead are buried there."

"This wasn't just their dead," Camille said, moving to sit next to him. "This was their criminals. They were violent." She put a hand on her husband's forearm, and she shifted to wrap his fingers around hers. "They were insane," she whispered, and both of them recalled the crazed look on the man who had clung to their ceiling only days before.

Brad sighed. "There's really only one thing we can do," he said, standing. Then he grinned down at Camille. "Luckily…we had a break in the market." Camille stared up at him, her mouth open. "We got it all back, babe. Everything we lost, and quite a bit more."

Chapter Nine

Brad and Camille stood at the edge of the lawn, looking up at the mansion. Camille's eyes followed the gorgeous curves and swoops of the woodwork. Brad was eyeing the branches of the oak that he could see over the top of the house, and the lilac bushes that were already beginning to bloom – despite there being two inches of snow still on the ground.

They had paid a moving company to pack everything up for them in one day, not willing to step foot in the house again. Camille would miss the huge office downstairs and the beautiful patio she'd been able to step onto. She hoped they could find somewhere similar, once they got the accounts straightened out and could put a new bid in somewhere.

They were taking a big loss on the house. The town had agreed to buy it from the couple and use it as a historical site. It would be used, the mayor assured them, as a local museum. They had more than enough history to display down in the basement of the library. It would all be dug out. And, he told them sheepishly, they'd even convinced some local tribesmen to come in and cleanse the area.

The man seemed embarrassed by the admission, but Brad sighed in relief. "If anything will get rid of the bad luck and the violence, it's that," he remarked to Camille as they left the town hall.

"I'm tempted to take a cutting," Camille said after following her husband's eyes to where he was staring at the lilacs. He looked at her quickly.

"Don't. I'll buy you a few bushes, I promise, wherever we end up."

She laughed and placed a hand on her stomach. There was nothing there yet, but she had plans for their future…for a family in a new home. "Don't worry. They're beautiful, but I don't think I could stand the scent of them anymore."

The couple would be moving temporarily to an apartment in the heart of the city, where they could work comfortably until they found a new home, hopefully a little closer to work. Neither one of them had really been satisfied with the home office setting. It had been fun while it lasted, but Brad preferred to be less distracted by baked goods, and Camille wanted a shorter commute to the office. She didn't plan on working for too long, as the doctor had warned her to take it easy on their second try.

"You ready?" Brad asked, turning his gaze away from the side yard. Camille took one last look at the house. It had been so close to everything they'd dreamed of, even if she didn't know she'd been dreaming of it. But now, she had more direction in her life.

"I am," she said, smiling up at her husband. He grinned back and took her hand, turning toward the SUV and the road that led to the city.

The End

More Books by Carrie Bates:

The Haunting of Thomas House

The Haunting of Maple Mansion

The Haunting of Hilltop Mansion

The Haunting of Whitfield Mansion

The Haunting of Owensboro Mansion

The Haunting of Maynard Mansion

The Haunting of Kessinger Mansion
The Haunting of Krakow Convent
The Haunting of St. Doyle Seminary
The Haunting of Skye Ocean Liner
The Haunting of Harper House

Printed in Great Britain
by Amazon